The Riot Act

by the same author

THE RIOT ACT

A version of Sophocles'
Antigone

TOM PAULIN

faber and faber
LONDON · BOSTON

First published in 1985
by Faber and Faber Limited
3 Queen Square London WC1N 3AU

Phototypeset by Wilmaset Birkenhead Merseyside
Printed in Great Britain by
Whitstable Litho Limited Whitstable Kent

British Library Cataloguing in Publication Data

Paulin, Tom
The riot act : a version of Sophocles' Antigone
I. Title   II. Sophocles. Antigone
822'.914   PR6066.A884

ISBN 0–571–13613–3

For Eric and Deirdre Brown

After the death of their father, Oedipus, Eteocles and
Polynices were to rule Thebes in alternate years, but
Eteocles would not give up his throne at the end of his year
of rule. This led to the expedition of the Seven against
Thebes, in which seven heroes fought bitterly to retain the
throne for Polynices. In a duel between Eteocles and
Polynices to decide the issue, the brothers killed each
other. Their uncle, Creon, became king of Thebes.

Creon orders that Eteocles be buried according to the
proper rites and customs, and he forbids the burial of
Polynices. It is the law of the gods that Antigone must
bury her brother's body. Ismene, Antigone's sister, though
she recognizes the imperative force of divine law, opposes
Antigone's decision.

Characters

ANTIGONE
ISMENE, her sister
CHORUS LEADER
CHORUS
CREON, King of Thebes
AIDE TO CREON (a member of the chorus)
GUARD
TWO GUARDS
HAEMON, Creon's son
TIRESIAS
BOY ATTENDANT
MESSENGER
EURYDICE, Creon's wife

The Riot Act was first presented by Field Day Theatre Company at the Guildhall, Derry, on 19 September 1984. The cast was as follows:

CHORUS	The Company
CHORUS LEADER	Ciarán Hinds
ANTIGONE	Veronica Quilligan
ISMENE	Hilary Reynolds
CREON	Stephen Rea
GUARD	Mark Lambert
HAEMON	Joe Crilly
TIRESIAS	Des McAleer
MESSENGER	Kilian McKenna
EURYDICE	Nuala Hayes

Directed by Stephen Rea
Designed by Brien Vahey
Music by Keith Donald
Lighting by Rory Dempster

An open space in front of the royal palace at Thebes. The palace has three doors; the central door is the largest. It is dawn, the morning after the deaths of Eteocles and Polynices and the flight of the Argive army. The stage is the grey of bedrock. Triangles, masonic symbols, neo-classical architrave.

ANTIGONE *looks over her shoulder quickly at the central door and takes* ISMENE *by the arm for a moment.*

ANTIGONE

Ismene, love,
my own sister,
you know there's a last bitterness
we've to taste yet?

ISMENE

What more could they tell me?
Have we a third brother we could
   lose?
Look, it's the stony ground, this –
you can pin no grievance on it.
(Pause, conceding)
   I heard, though,
   the Argives pulled out last night.

ANTIGONE

We all know that.
Stay quiet now
and I'll tell you.

ISMENE

What's fretting you?
They're both dead –
dead in the one day.
There's no worse grief than that.

9

Just listen and you'll know there is.
Eteocles will be buried
and buried right,
but Polynices,

(*Mimics, angry*)

     that traitor,
must lie exposed
on the barren ground.
And he says, our great Creon,
that the crows can pick
at his disloyal body –
as the rats and the rain will –
but no one may touch, bless
nor cover him over.
And you and me both,
we're expected to take this!
We must bend the knee
or they'll stone us in the street.
All I know's this –
we must put our own lives

(*Pointing down*)

     right there on the line
and show no fear of him.

ISMENE

But, love,
if that's his order
there's no way the likes of us
can make him change it.

ANTIGONE

Will you go in with me or not?

ISMENE

In where? In what?
What are you after?

ANTIGONE

I must bury him.
Will you help me do it?

ISMENE

You'd set him in the earth
when we both know
even touching him's outside the
    law?

ANTIGONE

He's my own brother,
and he's yours too.
I can't betray him.

ISMENE

You're talking wild –
it's Creon's order.

ANTIGONE

He's no right, ever,
to keep me from my own.

ISMENE

Look, sister,
just you remember
how Oedipus
our father died.
They turned on him
when he himself
found out what wrong he'd done.

It was our father
tore his own eyes out.
His mother – aye, and wife –
she hanged herself,
then our two brothers
ripped themselves apart.
Can you imagine, but,
what way *we'll* die? –
some screggy, smelly crowd,
us dragged before them –
oh they'll spit,
they'll sleg us then,
shout all the dirt
till the first stones go *whap*!
(*Smacks hands near Antigone's face*)
and go on thumping us.
Don't tell me it's not right –
that's what *is*!
Would you have me cry
for some great change
out there in nature?
(*Points at audience*)

ANTIGONE
I'll not persuade you.
You won't link hands with me,
not now, not ever.
That's your nature.
But I'll go bury him
and die for it,
though I've hurt no one.
My heart goes out
and honours them, our dead.
Stay you in the daylight
and keep his peace.

12

ISMENE

I have my piety
as well as you,
but the state's not putty
and I can't force it.

ANTIGONE

I love my brother
so I must bury him.
You'd dodge and run.

ISMENE

I'm frightened for you.

ANTIGONE

What way *you're* going,
that worries me.

ISMENE

Don't breathe a word then,
and I won't either.

ANTIGONE

The more blame you'll get
for lying quiet.

ISMENE

You burn for them,
but they're cold things, principles.

ANTIGONE

What thing ever I must do
there's one audience
(*Looks away from audience*)
will understand it.

ISMENE

You'll change nothing,
only make it worse.

ANTIGONE

I'll only do what's right
and sanctioned by the gods.

ISMENE

It's hardly worth it.

ANTIGONE

Ismene – sister –
don't make me hate you.
When you talk that way
it's like you're sour
on everything that's sacred.
Go you on back
and leave me here.
It's never pride,
not pride that's pushing me –
it's my own soul and honour
I can nor bend nor sell.

(*Exit* ANTIGONE *right.* ISMENE *goes into palace by one of the two side doors*)

CHORUS LEADER

Thebes has seven gates
and the sun shines on each one:
just take a look
at the triangle
and the compasses –
dead clear they are,
like an open book.

It's as clear as the day is long that Polynices was in the wrong.

His story was a thin wee grievance that went on for ages. He thrived on it, killed his brother and died complaining.

His brother, now, he was all for reason and this city. He died smiling.

The sun's shining now. Isn't it good to be here? And our enemies – they're in the dark just. They're ancient history.

Ah, but it's great to be shot of them!

CHORUS LEADER
Now watch the big man
this bran-new morning:
our new king Creon's
wanting some wise words
from us old ones.

(*Enter* CREON *from the central doors of the palace with two attendants. The chorus sit down in front of him and he addresses them, mostly looking over their heads but with occasional public smiles in their direction. Often he seems to be speaking purely for his own delight, savouring certain juicy vowels, whipping others into fine peaks.*)

CREON
Mr Chairman, loyal citizens of Thebes, these recent months have indeed been a most distressing time for us all. It therefore gives me great pleasure to report that public confidence and order are now fully restored, and, if I may, I would further like to take this opportunity of thanking each and every one of you for your steadfastness and your most exceptional loyalty. I know that Laius, when he was king, always counted on and received your full support. And again, during Oedipus's

reign and after his tragic death, your continued support for our state was very much appreciated.

Sadly, since that time both of Oedipus's sons have died in battle, and I'm sure I need not remind anyone here of the most unfortunate circumstances in which they died. For purely technical and legal reasons – kinship to the dead and so on – the office of king therefore devolves upon me. Such a position brings with it a very, very heavy responsibility, and it is probably true that no one who has not at some time or other assumed the burdens of public office can ever really reveal the full range of their abilities – or even, we may say, of their professional limitations.

For my own part, I have always held that one of the soundest maxims of good government is: *always listen to the very best advice.* And in the coming months I shall be doing a very great deal of listening, sounding opinions and so forth. However, let me say this, and say it plainly right at the very outset, that if ever any man here should find himself faced with a choice between betraying his country and betraying his friend, then he must swiftly place that friend in the hands of the authorities. That is the only right and proper decision and we must all abide by it.

If I might further add – and I know that Zeus will support me here – that if ever I should see this country heading for disaster I would be quite incapable of standing idly by and saying nothing. Nor could I conceive of having even the slightest personal friendship with anyone who wished my country ill. For we must at all times be vigilant and be prepared to speak up and lend a hand. If that should not be the case, then it would be most unwise to predict that our present peace and prosperity, with all the opportunities that accompany them, will last for very much longer.

These, in brief, are the principles by which I intend to govern this city. And it follows naturally from those same principles that I should wish to amplify the statement which was issued in my name yesterday evening. (*Puts on a pair of rimless spectacles and reads from a piece of paper which an aide hands him.*) 'Eteocles, who died fighting for his city, shall be given a full state funeral' – reversed arms, carriage and so on – 'whilst Polynices' – it was Polynices, you remember, who slipped into this country and tried to destroy our holy places – 'Polynices shall be deemed guilty of treason and refused all burial.' (*Removes spectacles*)

I have therefore decided that his remains are best left exposed in some distant but still public place away from our city. Eteocles, we may say, was exemplary, but of Polynices we must, most regrettably, make an example. It is in this spirit, and in this spirit alone, that I would wish to conduct all civic business here. And you may rest assured that anyone who breaks the law will be pursued with all the vigour that I can command, while those who uphold it can always count on my full support. Thank you all for coming, and any questions just now? We have one minute. (*Flashes stonewall smile*)

CHORUS LEADER
Creon, son of Menoecéus,
you've spelt the law out
and you can enforce it.

CREON
But I expect you
to do your duty too.

CHORUS LEADER

Why us, though?
there's younger men
would mind his body better.

CREON

Armed guards
are already in place.

CHORUS LEADER

What'd you have us do then?

CREON

You must, at all times,
lend no support
to anyone who breaks my laws.

CHORUS LEADER

Sure no one in their right mind
would choose to die.

CREON

(*Leaning over, in a soft growl*)
Money, brother –
dirty, dirty money –
might lead them by the nose.
(*Enter* GUARD)

GUARD

Your honour, I didn't run the whole way here – and if
I'm honest with myself I can't say I'm anyways puffed at
all – for I have to tell ye I kept stopping and thinking the
whole time, and a few times even I turned right round
and set off back again, for I just kept telling myself,
'Sammy, you're a fool, you're a complete eejit – aren't

you walking right into it? But then just suppose there's
someone else gets there first and tells him? Wouldn't it be
the worse for you, like?' So I kept stopping and starting
and dodging this way and that like a real loony . . . it took
me ages to get here, but in the end I just had to come and
tell you. I'm real sorry about this, and the only thing I can
say is: I done my duty and I must take what comes.

CREON

My good man,
pray tell me simply
what's on your tiny mind.

GUARD

Well, first I'd better explain that *I* didn't do it – oho, no –
and I didn't see who done it neither. So it's not right the
likes of me should carry the can for something they never
did in the first place – if you take my meaning.

CREON

That your hands are clean?
Clean of what, though?
Quick, man.

GUARD

Aye, well, is there anyone likes
breaking bad news?

CREON

(*Snapping fingers in his face*)
Now!

GUARD

OK, it's like this what happened – and it's the whole
truth this. There was dust – aye, dust – on the corp.

Someone had sprinkled it all over him and done all the
proper rites . . .

CREON
Name the man who'd dare to!

GUARD
(*Impatiently*) I can't . . . (*Continuing thread*) But there
wasn't the dunt of a pick nor shovel to be seen anywhere.
No earth had been turned, the ground was bone-hard –
no tracks nor footprints, nothing. Whoever done it just
vanished off the face of the earth. And when the relief
came and showed us – at the scrake of dawn just – it was
kind of a wonder, really. The dead man, he'd this fine
veil of dust all over him as though there was someone
really cared, someone who never just went through the
motions of doing the right thing by him and then skipped
off. And you know, there wasn't one sign any beast had
touched him – not a sign. He wasn't the least bit ripped
nor torn. It was wild, though – we just stared at him for a
long while, quiet-like, then [*zap!*] we were all screaming at
each other. There wasn't one person there would take the
blame. We all swore blind none of us knew what
happened, and we'd have gone through fire – gone every
one of us – just to prove it. In the end, like, we found
nothing and we'd to call the search off. But there was one
among us there spoke up – and then, boy, were we
frightened! But there was no way you could fault what he
said, nor let yourself off the hook neither, once you
followed his logic. What he said was we just better *had*
report the incident, and not chance for a cover-up.
Anyways, we drew lots, and me myself – I got the short
straw. I never wanted to leave the place. But I'm here,
and it's bad news all right.

CHORUS LEADER

Your majesty,
a word in your ear –
could the gods have done it?

CREON

Old man,
d'you know what they call that?
Blasphemy.
Don't let me hear it.
What god was it
took the least care of him ever?
Did he serve them right?
Was he loyal?
Didn't he march with fire
to burn their shrines
and break the law?
So tell me now –
the unjust, do the gods honour
    them?
Do they prosper?
No way. Never.
Don't talk now;
I know what's happened.
I mind the whole of it.
Right from the start
there was moaning,
fly men at the back
telling black lies about me –
egging the boys on
and flashing their money.
It's as clear as the day,
those guards were bought –
didn't I say money's dirt?
Dirt and nothing but?

So, before Zeus,
let me spell it out now:
(*To* GUARD *and half-imitating his accent when he gives the order*)

go you, dead quick,
and find who done it,
else I'll tear the skin
off o'the whole pack o'ye
and roast you real slow.

GUARD

Can I say something?

CREON

Your voice grates on me.

GUARD

Aye, does it sting your ears or your conscience?

CREON

Why – why should it?

GUARD

I may hurt your ears, but there's someone else has
bruised your soul.

CREON

You're a spieler only.

GUARD

That's as may be, but I done nothing.

CREON

You were bought, boy,
and you'll pay the price.

GUARD

You know, the likes of you – I never thought till now just
how wrong yous are.

CREON

You never thought!
Don't strain yourself,
a philosopher-guard
would make us all weep.
Don't stand there gawking –
go find him quick.

(*Exit*)

GUARD

I hope he's found. I hope so. But whether he is or not –
and the whole thing's chance from start to finish – you
won't catch this boy near the hot seat again. I never
thought for one minute he'd let me off. But he has, the
ould bugger, he has indeed. I'll see you.
(*Exit*)

CHORUS

There are many wonders on this earth
and man has made the most of them;
though only death has baffled him
he owns the universe, the stars,
sput satellites and great societies.

Fish pip inside his radar screens
and foals kick out of a syringe:
he bounces on the dusty moon
and chases clouds about the sky
so they can dip on sterile ground.

By pushing harder every way,
by risking everything he loves,
he makes us better, day by day:
we call this progress and it shows
we're damned near perfect!

(*Enter* GUARD *leading* ANTIGONE)

CHORUS LEADER

Maybe nature
or the gods are mad:
this girl's the daughter
of wrecked Oedipus.

GUARD

She is, aye. Where's the big noise?

CHORUS LEADER

(*Seeing* CREON *entering left behind* GUARD)
Creon is coming shortly.
We asked would he meet us:
it was very decent of him
to say *yes*.

CREON

Quick, what news have you?

GUARD

Your honour, I could've sworn blind you'd seen the last
of me entirely, but after I left here – well, I was dead
lucky. I feel grand now. Tell you the truth, I was that
scared by all you said . . . but that's no matter. I'd just
slipped over for a last look – thought I'd give it one
more try, I did – when: would you believe it? There's this
wee girl spreading the dust on him and pouring wine on

24

the ground. So I nabbed her straight. It's all me that done
it and no one else – there were no straws this time round
– not at all. So you can lock her up now and knock a
statement out of her. I'm glad to be rid of this bother.

CREON

Guard, you hold the prisoner.
It's you must give us
every last detail now.

GUARD

She was burying him! that's what.

CREON

Would you swear it in court?
Have you the facts straight?

GUARD

(*Wearily*) *Prisoner was apprehended while in the act of*
performing burial rites on the body of her brother, Polynices. Is
that clear enough?

CREON

Who was it observed her?
And by whom was the arrest made?

GUARD

OK, OK, if you want it in full, I'll tell you. And let me
take my time with it. We went back to the place – mind,
we were all dead scared after the sleggin' you'd given me
– anyway we went back and brushed all the dust off of
the corp. Soft and pobby he was, and he smelt rotten. He
was bare to the sky so we skipped up a big dune upwind
of him that give us a good view. We kept each other

and if anyone nodded off you can bet your boots they were
rudely wakened. We stayed that way till the sun was high
and the heat lay on us like a board. It was then the wind
blew up and suddenly – *trouble!* – we were lost in this huge
dust-storm and the entire place was obliterated. We could
see nothing. It was like the gods had chosen that moment
to put the boot in. Real neat it was and there was nothing
we could do about it. And then, after a long long while, the
storm started slacken. I peeked my head up and there
she was, crying out like a plover – a stinty kind of a cry that
stuck in your ears – and skipping this way and that like
she'd lost her wains. But the curses she threw out! You
should have heard her. Then she went and sprinkled dust
on him, lifted a brass jug – a thin wee jug, it was – and
poured the libations, once, twice, three times. Once we
seen that we rushed down on her and grabbed her. She
denied nothing, didn't show the least fear neither. It was a
relief, I can tell you. I was real pleased – for myself, like –
for I knew I was off the hook. Still and all, it's hard to book
one of your own. But I'm in the clear now and that's all
that matters.

CREON

(*To* ANTIGONE *who is staring at the ground*)
You there –
dirt-watcher –
d'you deny it?

ANTIGONE

No, why should I?

CREON

(*To* GUARD)
Skip off, you.
Your hands are clean.

(*To* ANTIGONE)
    You knew the law?

ANTIGONE
It was a public statement
and I heard it.

CREON
So you set out –
it was deliberate –
to cross your own king?
Your uncle too?

ANTIGONE
It was never Zeus
made that law.
Down in the dark earth
there's no law says,
'Break with your own kin,
go lick the state.'
We're bound to the dead:
we must be loyal to them.
I had to bury him.

CHORUS
It's in her blood:
she won't surrender
the least point in Creon's favour.

CREON
They're easy broken
that yap like this one.
If she were a man, now,
she'd maybe stick.

(To guards)
> Bring little sister
> and we'll spike the pair of them.

ANTIGONE
You'd do more than murder.
I can tell it by your eyes.

CREON
Just being rid of you
'll satisfy me.

ANTIGONE
What are you waiting on?
You heard me say it –
I had to bury him.
Though they're keeping quiet,
the people know that.

CREON
You're out on your own.
No one in Thebes
will follow you, ever.

ANTIGONE
D'you hear the hush?
They're only waiting.

CREON
I hear nothing.
You should be ashamed.

ANTIGONE
I stuck by my brother –
where's the shame in that?

CREON

And hadn't you a brother
on the other side died?
He knew the difference
between right and wrong.

ANTIGONE

He'd the same mother
and the same father too.

CREON

So he'd never tell you
there's not the least scrap
of piety –
real honest piety –
in what you've done?

ANTIGONE

That he'd never do.

CREON

Not though you levelled him
with a state traitor?

ANTIGONE

They were full brothers.
They were equal.

CREON

(*Pointing to gates and wall*)
It was *this* he would defend:
the other, he would've burnt it.

ANTIGONE

That's no great matter now
to either one.

They're gone from this
and must be buried right.

CREON

So the good,
they're equal-levelled with the bad?

ANTIGONE

Who knows but that the dead
can lie in peace together?

CREON

What we loathe in our own lifetime
stays with us after death.

ANTIGONE

It's not my nature,
I can't rip myself with hate.
I love the pair of them.

CREON

You can join them then.
As long as I draw breath
I'll not be bested by a woman.
(*Enter* ISMENE *from the palace, led by two attendants*)
And this one here –
the sneaky, sleaked one –
she lived in my house too.
A pair of beetles
that ground good mortar
into dust.
(*To* ISMENE)
Tell us the truth now:
it was you helped her.

ISMENE

Aye, from the start I backed her.
We were in it both –
(*Nodding at* ANTIGONE)
she'll tell you.
(CREON *watches, sometimes impassive, sometimes looking from one to the other in a manner that is vigilant, cynical, judicial*)

ANTIGONE

You'd no hand in it at all.

ISMENE

Why d'you throw me off?
I'm sticking with you.

ANTIGONE

As the dead are my witness,
I went out on my own.

ISMENE

Sister, don't chuck me over.
I'll go die with you;
respect the dead I will.

ANTIGONE

We'll not split this death.
The one sacrifice is enough.

ISMENE

And how could I bide here
with you gone?

ANTIGONE

(*Jerking her head casually at* CREON)
You may ask Creon that:
deep down, it's him you care for.

ISMENE

Quit saying that.
You're wronging me.

ANTIGONE

I have to tell you;
it tears my heart, though.

ISMENE

Can you not listen?
I'm with you the whole way.

ANTIGONE

Save your own skin.
I wouldn't blame you.

ISMENE

I will not. Never.
I'll go with you instead
and take what happens.

ANTIGONE

Get by, put up with things:
it was your choice, that.
My choice destroys me.

ISMENE

You might have heeded
what I told you then.
It's the least bit thing
I tried to make you.

ANTIGONE

A whole huge world
gave you a soft pat for that.

A deeper one knows why
I couldn't heed you.

ISMENE

I crossed over to you.
I must be guilty now.

CREON

(*To* ISMENE)
So little sister
has turned vicious too?

ANTIGONE

Take heart, love;
just live your life.
I've been dedicated
this long while.

ISMENE

I was cautious once
and made no bother.

CREON

You lost the head
when you followed her.

ISMENE

Could I stand living here
without she shared the pain?

CREON

Don't talk of sharing.
She's dead to both of us.

ISMENE

You'd slay the girl
your son would wed?

CREON

There's plenty more
that he can poke.

ISMENE

He loves her only
and he will do always.

CREON

A hard bitch like that!
I'll let no son of mine
go near it.

ANTIGONE

Oh Haemon, love,
he'd tear your heart!

CREON

Quiet! Quiet here!

CHORUS

You'd really take her
from your own son?

CREON

She chose to leave us.

CHORUS

It's fixed, your sentence?

Aye, it's fixed.

(*To guards*)

Go on, boys,
and fetch them to the house.
Let them cry whatever.
They belong there.

(*Exit guards with* ISMENE *and* ANTIGONE. CREON *remains, thinking, oblivious to* CHORUS)

CHORUS LEADER

(*Addressing* CHORUS) Ever since the day I first made this speech – it was in another time and place, and in a different language too – the grief I was speaking of then has grown and multiplied. It's got more and more.

What I'd say now is simply this – the world is a very, very old place, but the people in it, they're very young still, and if you've never grieved then you're lucky.

Generation after generation has suffered, and every time we think to get free of what happened before and will surely happen after, then we find there's something in our road, like a ramp maybe, that we can never get over, that we can never push past.

So we give up because we know it's taking us nowhere.

CHORUS

There was a man I knew
got footless at his own wedding.
Covered in blood he was.

CHORUS LEADER

Now Antigone must die.
I ask you is it worth it
for a handful of dust on Polynices?

(*Enter* HAEMON)

35

He's maybe angry, Haemon?

CREON
We'll soon know it.
(*To* HAEMON)
> Son, there's only one sentence
> and it's the just one.
> Would you fling stones
> at your own father?
> Or will you stick with me
> no matter?

HAEMON
Look, father,
I'm your own flesh and blood.
Haven't I shown it always
by doing what you bid me?
If I married out
or quit the house,
I'd get no blessing from you.

CREON
Obey your father,
that's only nature.
If we've no law,
nor right discipline,
there's no trust neither.
I've seen children
chuck both parents over –
blood on the walls
and the whole street laughing!
I've watched good men wrecked
by some hard-nosed bitch –
get stuck with that kind,

there's no joy there.
So let me tell you
I'll not back down.
I made that law –
the law is clear;
she broke it,
on her head be it.
She betrayed the state
and she betrayed me:
it would vindicate her
if she got off free.
No, you'll find I'm tougher
nor a shrieking woman.

CHORUS LEADER
You're right there.
That's a wise man talking
or I'm a born eejit.

HAEMON
The gods, father,
they made us reasonable.
Don't think I'm saying
that it's wrong, your law,
but listen, listen, please,
to what's going happen
if you stick firm.
Would I be your son
if I never heeded
what's yacking in the streets?
I tell you, they're scared no more –
not scared of you.
Something's turned them.
'Thon girl did right',
'What wrong's she done?' –

37

it's that they're saying.
'If there was justice here,
she'd get the praise then –
she'd be honoured for it.'
That's the whisper
and it's catching on
like sticky fire.
But father,
you're dearest to my heart:
all you've done I'm proud of,
I care for it.
Still, there's no one can be right
day in, day out.
We make mistakes, get lucky,
by learning from them.
It's madness, though,
to go so far, far out
you'll hark to no man.
Be firm sometimes,
then give a bit – that's wise.
You don't back down,
just go with the tide,
then ride it tight.
So, put by your anger –
I'm your son,
just listen to me.
You won't regret it.

CHORUS LEADER
He might be right, your honour,
though mind you,
there's a power of truth
in what you told him.

CREON

Am I to go to my books again?
Is he the master?

HAEMON

If I read you a lesson,
don't mind the tone of it.
Just brood on what I said.

CREON

It's a brave fine thing, then,
to back a rebel?

HAEMON

I never said that.

CREON

I fed and clothèd her:
she bit the hand o' me.

HAEMON

The people of Thebes
would contradict you.

CREON

You'd have them tell me
what laws I'll make?

HAEMON

You never listened.

CREON

Or split my rule, then,
with some king else?

HAEMON

That's no city
where one man only
holds all the power.

CREON

It's mine by right.

HAEMON

Put your throne in a desert:
you'll burn yourself.

CREON

You'd take a woman's side?

HAEMON

I'm only telling you what's right.

CREON

You've no respect then.
To turn on me like this
out here in public!

HAEMON

You broke the law.

CREON

But the law – I made it!
It's written down.
I'm sticking by it.

HAEMON

There's a higher law –
aye, a deeper one –
and that you stuck a hole in.

CREON

The sleaked creature
that you are!
He's given in –
and to a *woman!*

HAEMON

Where there's injustice
I can't stay quiet.

CREON

You back her cause
with every word you utter.

HAEMON

And yours, and mine –
the gods below must know it.

CREON

You'll never bed with her;
not in this life, never.

HAEMON

If she should come to harm,
then someone else will.

CREON

You'd threaten me?

HAEMON

No threat:
it's what I know must happen.

CREON

Then you'll be sorry for it.

HAEMON

If you weren't my father,
I'd go tell all Thebes
what wrong you've done.

CREON

Just listen to her!

HAEMON

You'd speak, you'd mock;
but you never, never listen.

CREON

(*Wild*)

D'you say so?
D'you say so?
By the gods in heaven
you'll bite that flitchy tongue.
Bring out the dirty bitch
and let's be rid of her.

HAEMON

Shout on, old man,
there's no one here
dare harm her now.
I'll see they don't.

(*Exit*)

CREON

I'll make him hear
her every scream,
I'll tear the shite
from out the pair of them!

CHORUS

Your honour,
who knows what he may do?
I wouldn't push him.

CREON

No threat in that one.
Those pair must die, but.

CHORUS

You'd kill them both?

CREON

No, not both of them, you're right.
Her hands are clean.

CHORUS

And the other girl,
what thing'll happen her?

CREON

Let her be taken out,
out to the far ridge.
Caves I've seen there
with sheep-dirt in them.
Find the deepest one there is,
leave bread and olives
and some drinking water –
then wall her in.
She can pray to the dark mould,
make gods of it if she wants to.

(*Exit*)

CHORUS LEADER

It's love has done this. Love's responsible. But what is it,
love, would you tell me?

43

You've seen the air tremble on a hot day – a clemmed
shimmer, like chains?

You've seen a wide snowy field when it's dayligone
and the sky violet?

You've seen a dead light on the sea of astronomers? A
bruised peach, blood-orange – a padded cell, a frazzled
moth? – aye, well, you've known love.

CHORUS LEADER

But she's going out to die, and no tears shed.

CHORUS

Slip and slime, skin and fur, a rough shove in the night –
that's love.

(ANTIGONE *is brought out of palace by two guards*)

CHORUS LEADER

I look at her, Antigone, and the heart in me's torn.

ANTIGONE

(*To* CHORUS)

> People of Thebes,
> it's a fine day for a wedding,
> let me take a last look
> at the sun shining.

CHORUS

> Sure we'll write about you.
> A poem, a song or two –
> no one else stood out the same –
> will celebrate you.

ANTIGONE

There were others like me.
Niobe, I heard it said,
was turned to stone.

(*Sings half to herself*)

'One day early I went out
to climb a hill like a pig's back,
and as the rain began to spit
I heard her cry it was my hard luck.'

CHORUS

That one was a goddess, but.
You'd need be dead famous
to have them set your name next
    hers.

ANTIGONE

You can't wait
till I'm buried can you?
This city's sacred to me,
but you'd sneer at anyone
would love, yet leave it.

CHORUS

You went out to the far edge,
put your own life on the line;
maybe, though, it's your father's
    crimes
that you're paying for?

ANTIGONE

Say it straight out, then –
their bed stank;
they made us there –
we came screaming

from the same blood.
Ah, Polynices,
your wedding meant war;
it's your death has sent me
out to die this day.

You did your duty
by your dead brother,
but no one crosses
the likes of Creon.
You were stubborn always
and that's destroyed you.

ANTIGONE

(*Sings to herself*)
              'I heard her cry
              as I climbed the track –
              my friends are cold
              though my bairns are dead.'
(*Enter* CREON)

CREON

Who'd guess
that one wick song
has never stayed
the hangman's hand?
(*To guards*)
              Get out of this
              and shut her from the light;
              she belongs in the dark
              like any blacky.

46

(*Sings, musing*)

       '. . . my friends are cold
       though my bairns are dead.'

(*Walks forward*)

       Laius, Oedipus, Jocasta,
       Eteocles and Polynices,
       I call on you, my kin –
       may you bid me welcome
       where I'm going now;
       and let the gods witness
       that I broke no law.
       If there's fault with me,
       I'll soon know it.
       But if I'd a husband
       or a child even
       and they dead, dead but not buried,
       I'd have laid no earth on them
       if the law forbade me.
       And why? It's simple.
       I might wed some other man,
       have child by another,
       but no one, now,
       can make me a new brother.
       So I must honour him
       and die unwed.
       I'm bound to him
       as he to me –
       break what's between us
       and there's neither love,
       nor honour, left.

CHORUS

Wild as ever
in her speech she is.

CREON

Her guards can listen;
the dark may too.

ANTIGONE

(*Shivers slightly; the guards move in on her*)
City of my fathers
and you gods of ours,
oh, watch them take me.
I loved, and feared the gods –
tell me that wasn't wrong.

(ANTIGONE *is led away quickly by the guards. The* CHORUS
LEADER *begins before she has disappeared.*)

CHORUS LEADER

That yarn about Danae, we all know how lovely she was
– her face shone, she was that beautiful – but her father
was told she'd bear a son that would rise and kill him. So
he built her a house out of hard rock and put a door in it
with thick brass nails, and he kept her there, locked up,
all on her own.

She was a proud girl – every bit proud, daughter, as
you are now – and she came of a long line of kings,
which was why the great Zeus turned himself into a
shower of rain and dropped into her lap like a clatter of
gold sovereigns that have been rubbed fresh, like new.
And then, the bold Zeus, he swam in a bit further. So she
bore the son.

It may be desperate, but we can none of us escape our
fate – neither good clean money, nor weapons, nor a
city's walls, nor great strong ships, can stop what must
happen us. It's daft to hope otherwise.

Lycurgus, he disliked music and strong drink, and
when the crack was good he was bitter. He was a neat
kind of a punctual man, and he annoyed Dionysus, for he

liked neither a slow air nor an ould tune; but there are
muses love the flute, and for he turned his back on them
he became sort of a hollow shell, more like a prison cell
than someone living.

There was a daughter of Boreas that's lord of the
winds, Cleopatra her name was, who married Phineus,
bore him two sons and then was cast off and put in
prison. Phineus, he took a second wife, and she got this
sharp shuttle, found the two sons and took them out
walking on the strand one night. Then she hacked their
eyes out.

That daughter of Boreas, she was brought up safe right
in the eye of the storm – the gods loved her – but the
Fates came and took her in the end. They're as old as the
hills, they're grey as stone, and they've found you, my
dear daughter, they've taken you away from me, so I'll
never see your face, never catch that voice, your voice
again, ever.

(*Enter* TIRESIAS, *led by a boy*)

TIRESIAS
It took time, getting here.
One pair of eyes between us.

CREON
You've a message, have you?

TIRESIAS
Aye, I've a message.
You may listen close.
I'll not repeat it.

CREON
Did I turn a deaf ear ever?

49

TIRESIAS

No, and this city
was the better for it.

CREON

I know we're grateful:
the whole place is.

TIRESIAS

Mark what I say then:
you're right on the edge.

CREON

It bothers me
what way you're talking.

TIRESIAS

(*A flinty chant in places*)

Then heed my art.
I climbed a hill,
the sun was hot,
my breath got short.
I had to tell
what's waiting on us;
to finger guts
and poke at shite –
that's evidence.
A bird scritched someplace –
that was strange
and then a clack of choughs
flew at each other;
I found my lair.
I set a fire for sacrifice
and laid flesh on it,
but would it catch?

Not anyhow.
Instead some fat
spat in the flames
and stank the place –
my rites had failed;
there was a greasy
sickness in the air.
Creon, you were too tough;
the state is dead.
That girl's brother,
he'd no right burial
and now his body
stinks on our altars,
stinks in our homes too.
The birds have tasted blood
from out his veins –
it's in their cries.
They sting my ears
and the gods, they'll hear no
    prayers.
Creon, you maimed him twice –
that's never right.
You'll pay the price.

CREON

They all pick faults in me.
What we don't want,
that's easy said –
not what we'd stick to.
Old man, old shaman,
just spit it out –
what bribe d'you take?

TIRESIAS

Is there anyone knows . . .

51

CREON

Knows what?

TIRESIAS

. . . that good advice
hurts only those
that lack the mother-wit
to take or recognize it?

CREON

No fool like an old fool.

TIRESIAS

You'd scoff and sneer
and say my words are paid for?

CREON

You prophets,
you're such blind
and webby things:
I've never known such people
for holding out their hands.

TIRESIAS

You rake the taxes
like any tyrant.

CREON

Whichever tune we choose,
the piper must be paid.

TIRESIAS

Did you heed me,
you'd save Thebes.

CREON

You're a wise man,
I know that.
But the side you've taken
it's worse than wicked.

TIRESIAS

(*As if he's heard something*)
There's a fear in me:
just by your talking
you quick the shape of it.

CREON

Go on, then, tell us.
My pocket's empty.

TIRESIAS

Aye, and your head too.

CREON

(*Moving closer*)
And know this, friend –
you'll not persuade me.
Never.

TIRESIAS

Listen, then go your way.
Let slip a few short days
and that strong lad you sired
will crack on a greased pyre.
While she was yet alive
you walled her in a cave;
his body you let ret
with neither prayer, nor rite.
Now so much blood's been spilt

there's none can call a halt
to those thrawn and jaggy hates
deep-rooted in your state.

(*Motioning with hand*)

Take me home, boy.
It's no use telling him.

(*Exit* TIRESIAS *with boy*)

CHORUS

Your honour, see that old man –
he's never yet been wrong.
I'm frightened for you.

CREON

(*To himself*)

Put on the kid gloves
else the gods'll scam me.

CHORUS

They'll worse than scam you.

CREON

What'd you have me do then?

CHORUS LEADER

Let the girl go free,
and rest him in his grave.

CREON

Back down, you're saying?

CHORUS LEADER

You've still got time.

CREON

(*Conceding*)

> We can't fight nature.
> It grates, but.

CHORUS

> Go quick now.
> Just you and no one else.

CREON

(*To guards*)

> Boys, go build the pyre –
> you can be gentle
> with his body now.
> Antigone, I'll set her free.
> It's best we keep that custom.

CHORUS LEADER

Zeus, the bold god you are, loud as the clouds cracking, quick as the lightning.

You watch over the Italian plains and you bid every guest welcome to the slippery great mysteries.

The grape's wild god – you're Bacchus, held for sacred in the city of Thebes, you are.

You live by the silky river, on holy ground the dragon's teeth were sown in.

Where you are there's no knowing: in the pitchy spit of pinewood burning, in the quick of tongues plunging – aye, in the greasy goat dance, the burst welt of a grape skin – you belong and you sing in them all.

Come heal us here, bring peace, come help us celebrate your names.

(*Enter* MESSENGER)

MESSENGER

Those of us who live here in the city that Cadmus and Amphion built know there's nothing fixed nor certain in this life.

Take Creon now – that man, he wanted for nothing, he'd everything you could want. He saved his country from its enemies, shared power with no man, had lovely children.

There was nothing and no one that wasn't under his thumb.

But that's all gone now. And d'you know why? I'll tell you.

He could neither bend nor listen. He held firm just that shade too long. There was no joy nor give in him ever. (*Glimpse of* EURYDICE *through partly opened doors*)

CHORUS

Scrap the sermon, boy.
Just tell us what happened.

MESSENGER

There's blood, I'm saying.
Aye, and guilt too.

CHORUS

So? Who died?
Who killed them?
Would you tell us?

MESSENGER

Haemon's dead.

CHORUS

Who killed him?

MESSENGER

He killed himself.
It was this mad anger
at his father made him.

CHORUS

The blind one saw it all.

MESSENGER

You're right to say it.
But there's worse yet.
(EURYDICE *enters slowly from one of the partly opened side doors*)

CHORUS

(*Backing off*)
You'll maybe tell her?
The queen, she'd want to hear you.

EURYDICE

(*To* MESSENGER *in a dazed voice*)
I was just leaving –
a prayer to Pallas,
it needed saying.
But I heard you speak
and fell back down.
Please break it here.
I'm ready now.

MESSENGER

Dearest lady,
I have to tell you
just like it happened –
you'll understand me.
For I was with your husband

out on the plain there,
out in the bad sun.
Way far we went,
walking till we found his body –
ah, Polyneices,
you were chewed by dogs
and never pitied!
So we prayed to her,
the goddess of the roads –
we asked that Pluto
would hold off a day.
And then we washed him,
took olive branches
and green laurel leaves
to crown and lap him in –
we burnt him then.
Next, we dug his native earth
and raised a mound;
a high, big mound
for all to see.
We never stopped –
that brave wee girl
was waiting on us:
she must be found.
But then – ack,
for the love of all that's holy
we heard such cries
and the king, your husband,
gave out this groan:
'That's Haemon, fetch,
go find him in the grave!
Oh quick, go find him now!
don't let the gods
play tricks on me.'
So we went and found them.

A desperate sight.
Antigone was dead –
she'd hung herself –
and Haemon, he was holding her,
dead gentle in his arms.
I have to tell you,
though Creon's face was japped
your son came spitting,
stabbed at him with his sword,
then turned
and dagged it in himself.
Poor lad, he's with her now.
They loved each other.

(EURYDICE *goes into the palace*)

CHORUS

She turned her back on you.
She said nothing.

MESSENGER

It's peace she needs –
just peace to grieve in.
Well, I'd like to think it.

(*Exit*)

CHORUS

And I would too.

(*Enter* CREON *with guards, carrying the shrouded body of* HAEMON *on a bier*)

CREON

Pity me, if you can.
Blind and thick,
a wretched, sinful man.

CHORUS

It was too late
you changed your mind.

CREON

(*Touching his son*)
      I changed it, but.
      Aye, changed it utterly.
(*Kneeling down*)
      Son, what god was it
      that sent me wild?
      And, son,
      how ever did I harm you?
      How could I do that
      my own wee man?
(*Enter* MESSENGER *from the palace*)

MESSENGER

Your honour, believe me,
I'd wish no more could happen you.

CREON

I'm burnt:
you couldn't singe me.

MESSENGER

Your queen is dead.
She killed herself.

CREON

No mercy, then.
O gods of hell,
try pity me.

(*To* MESSENGER)
>Show me, son.
>I'll quit from this.

CHORUS
>She's there;
>in there she is.

(*Doors of the palace are opened and the body of* EURYDICE *is displayed*)

CREON
>The bairn,
>and then the mother followed him.

MESSENGER
>She took a knife;
>she cursed you
>for a double killer.

CREON
>I am the man.
>Will no one take a sword
>and waste me now?
>I'm thick with sin.

MESSENGER
>It was right bitter
>the blame she laid on you.

CREON
>She stabbed herself?
>There was no one by
>that helped her go?

MESSENGER

By the altar:
she cut herself
again, and then again.

CREON

The full guilt's mine.
Show me the door just,
then chuck this dead one out.
Let it come, aye, let it come.
I want no light at all.

CHORUS

We've had enough
of dying in this place.

CREON

All I want's the dark.

CHORUS

Pray no more, Creon.
For you must bide
by what the gods have set.

CREON

Then put me out,
I'm begging you.

(*To himself*)

Wicked, cack-handed,
that's Creon.
Made a right blood-mess,
did Creon.
And where's the end of it?
Ask Creon.

(*As he is led away, the* CHORUS LEADER *speaks the closing lines*)

CHORUS LEADER

There is no happiness, but there can be wisdom.
Revere the gods; revere them always.
When men get proud, they hurl hard words, then
suffer for it.
Let them grow old and take no harm yet: they still get
punished.
It teaches them. It teaches us.